Digging DEEP

BY JAKE MADDOX

text by Wendy L. Brandes
illustrated by Katie Wood

STONE ARCH BOOKS
a capstone imprint

Jake Maddox Girl Sports Stories are published by Stone Arch Books
a Capstone imprint
1710 Roe Crest Drive
North Mankato, Minnesota 56003
www.mycapstone.com

**Library of Congress Cataloging-in-Publication Data is available
on the Library of Congress website.**

ISBN: 978-1-4965-6356-9 (library binding)
ISBN: 978-1-4965-6358-3 (paperback)
ISBN: 978-1-4965-6360-6 (ebook PDF)

Summary: Asiyah Najjar is upping her volleyball game and joining
the travel team. But the practices are longer, harder, and more
frequent than her old rec squad's. Now easygoing Asiyah is having
a tough time focusing and making the commitment. Can she
dig deep and jump to the next level of play?

Designers: Ted Williams and Laura Manthe
Production Specialist: Tori Abraham
Design Elements: Shutterstock

Printed and bound in Canada.
PA020

TABLE OF CONTENTS

CHAPTER ONE

Travel Team?

Asiyah Najjar and Lucy Stone were cracking up. They were eating lunch at school and were laughing so hard that they both almost fell out of their seats.

"You are the funniest person ever!" Lucy exclaimed. "You always make me laugh."

"We definitely have a lot of fun together," Asiyah replied.

"We'll have even more fun if we make the travel volleyball squad this year," Lucy said. "You are trying out tomorrow, right?"

Asiyah groaned. "Ugh, maybe? I'm not even sure if I want to join."

"Why not?" Lucy said, picking up a french fry. "I know you're not as excited about it as I am. But we'll improve so much. We'll play against better teams."

"I don't know. I like the old rec league where anyone could play," Asiyah said. "I don't think I'm competitive enough for travel volleyball."

"You're a good player. You'll be fine," Lucy replied. "Plus, you've gotten so much taller since last year. You could play in a bunch of different spots."

"I guess. It's just that travel teams have so many practices! When will I have time for piano lessons, or time just to relax?" Asiyah said.

She paused. "And on the town team, I didn't have to explain to anyone about wearing my hijab. The coaches and the players understood what it is and why I wear it."

Lucy looked at Asiyah's bright, flowered headscarf. "No one will care that you wear a hijab. Lots of Muslim girls wear them in all kinds of sports," she replied. "You have the skills to make the team. Try out!"

"I guess if I didn't make it, I'd just be back on the rec team," Asiyah said.

"So you'll do it? Are we are going to be travel-team buddies?" Lucy asked.

Asiyah put both thumbs up. Then she did a little dance, wriggling in her seat and whipping her head around. The two girls burst out laughing again.

CHAPTER TWO

A New Level

The next day, Asiyah and her older brother, Rad, walked to the town rec center. That's where the Lakeville Panthers travel team was having its tryout.

"Come on, Asiyah," Rad said. "You don't want to be late for tryouts."

Asiyah sighed and walked faster. "I'm not totally sure the travel team is even right for me," she told her brother.

"It could be really great," Rad said. "You know how much I love my travel soccer team. It's tough work, but it's worth it."

Soon they reached the rec center. Rad opened the door for his sister. They could hear the coach talking in the gym.

"Oh no, I *am* late!" Asiyah exclaimed.

Rad laughed. "Good luck, Asiyah!" he yelled as his sister rushed inside.

Asiyah scanned the gym and found Lucy sitting on the floor. Asiyah hurried over and plopped down next to her friend.

"I'm so glad you decided to come!" Lucy whispered.

Asiyah made a goofy face, and Lucy giggled quietly.

"You have to stop being so funny, or we'll get kicked out of tryouts!" Lucy said.

Asiyah smiled. "Fine, I'll stop. For now!" she whispered back.

They listened as Coach Elise talked. But soon Asiyah was looking around.

"Hey, Lucy! It's Shivani, Rachel, and Jessica from our old team," Asiyah whispered. She waved to her friends.

"We need to pay attention," Lucy said.

"Oh, right. Sorry!" Asiyah replied. She turned back to the coach.

"Players on this team rely on each other," Coach Elise said. "They push themselves because they want the team to succeed."

Asiyah sat up straighter. She still wasn't sure about travel volleyball, but the coach did make it sound exciting.

After Coach Elise finished her talk, she asked the girls to come to the net. "I'm going to hit a ball over," she said. "Tip, bump, or spike it back."

Asiyah was the first to go. As the ball came, she jumped high. She brought her hand down for the spike. But she hit the side of the ball. It dropped softly over the net.

"Try again," Coach told her.

This time, Asiyah was able to hit the ball a little harder. But it still fell weakly toward the sidelines. *I'll have to do better than that!* she thought.

Lucy was next. She was shorter than Asiyah. When she jumped, she didn't go as high, but she smacked the ball deep into the court.

After each girl had a few turns, Coach Elise blew her whistle. "Next, let's return some serves."

The girls lined up behind Asiyah in the back of the court. The coach served the ball.

Whoosh! The ball zoomed over the net.

Asiyah lunged for it. She put her hands together and bumped the ball into the air—then she landed on the floor with a splat!

"Yikes! That's the fastest ball I've ever seen," Asiyah told Lucy as she got back in line. "That serve twisted me into a pretzel!"

Lucy smiled. "You handled it pretty well, though."

Asiyah watched as her friends from the rec team stepped up. Shivani, Rachel, and Jessica easily returned Coach Elise's serves. Soon Asiyah got used to the speed too. On her third turn, she bumped it back—without doing a face plant.

By the time the tryout was done, Asiyah was tired and sore. She and Lucy gathered their things and started walking home.

"Phew! That was a lot of volleyball!" Asiyah exclaimed.

"Yeah, those drills were tough," Lucy said.

"I was kind of awkward at the beginning," Asiyah added. "But it felt awesome once I got the hang of returning Coach's serves."

"I think you have a really good chance of making the team," Lucy said.

"I know you will. You were great, like always!" Asiyah said.

"Well, we'll find out tomorrow," Lucy replied. "I can't wait until Coach Elise posts the list!"

Do I want my name to be on the roster? Asiyah thought as they walked. *It could be fun. But I might not be good enough. And it might be too much work!*

CHAPTER THREE

The Panthers

Asiyah's phone rang the next day while she was practicing piano. She checked her phone's display. It was Lucy.

I bet she's calling about the travel team, Asiyah thought. Her stomach twisted as she hit answer. *Am I good enough to make it?*

"We're both on the team!" Lucy shouted. "Coach Elise just posted the roster."

"Really? Woo-hoo! I'm doing my happy dance with two thumbs-up," Asiyah replied.

"Shivani, Jessica, and Rachel from our old team also made it," Lucy said.

"Awesome! That'll be so fun. So will practice start next week?" Asiyah asked.

"No, silly. Practice starts tomorrow," Lucy replied. "We have one every day after school this week. We can walk over together. This will be great, I promise. Two thumbs-up!"

"Four thumbs-up!" Asiyah said.

Lucy laughed. "See you tomorrow!"

Asiyah felt more excited about the Panthers than she thought she would. *I'll get to play with all my friends. Maybe it won't be so different from the old team after all.*

* * *

The next day, Asiyah and Lucy went into the gym. They spotted their old teammates.

"Hey, guys!" Asiyah shouted. She ran over and gave everyone a big hug.

"Asiyah! I'm so glad you made the team," Rachel said.

"Yeah, you always make practices fun!" Shivani added.

"I sure hope *these* practices will be fun too," Asiyah said. "Because they're going to last so much longer than our old team's practices."

The girls were still chatting when Coach Elise walked in. She blew her whistle, and the team gathered around.

"Welcome to the Lakeville Panthers!" the coach said. "You were all chosen because I believe you have the skills to be successful on this team."

Asiyah and Lucy smiled at each other.

"You'll notice big changes between rec volleyball and travel volleyball. You'll be learning new positions. And you'll be working extremely hard," Coach Elise said. "Your teammates will depend on you to give it your all during practices and games."

"Gulp," Asiyah said lightly.

The girls around her giggled.

When Coach Elise finished, the team went out onto the court. They lined up.

"First is the warm-up," Coach said. "We'll practice getting to the net and lightly tapping the ball over."

The girls took turns running forward. Coach bumped the ball over, and they tried to tip it back. When they did it right, the ball would gently fall close to the other side of the net.

Asiyah got ready for her turn. She rushed toward the net and jumped really high. She raised her hand and tried to tap the ball. But she pushed too hard. The ball went deep into the court.

"Try to keep your fingers together, Asiyah. But that's a good effort," Coach Elise said. "Keep going, girls. We're going to repeat this drill until everyone gets comfortable."

Asiyah went to the back of the line. As she got behind Lucy, she wobbled her knees.

"The same thing over and over? My legs are going to turn to jelly!" Asiyah said, expecting a laugh from her teammate.

Instead, Lucy sighed. "I might need to do this all day and night just to get it right. I wish I was tall like you. Then jumping high enough would be so much easier."

Asiyah stood up straight. "You'll get better at it," she said.

"Maybe, but it won't happen magically," Lucy said. "It's going to take a lot of hard work."

Asiyah didn't reply. Lucy was taking this way too seriously. *Sports are supposed to be fun,* she thought. *If we're working so hard, we should at least be enjoying it.*

CHAPTER FOUR

Dance Party

A few days later, Asiyah and Lucy were hanging out in Asiyah's room.

Asiyah took out her phone. "Oh, Luce, you have to see this music video. Look at the way the singer spins. She's amazing!"

Asiyah turned the volume up. She and Lucy stood and danced to the upbeat music. They giggled the whole time.

"Let's try to do that move," Asiyah said.

Both girls twirled around and around. Soon they were falling to the floor, laughing.

Their dance party was interrupted by a knock on the door. Rad poked his head in.

"Hey, Asiyah. Mom and Dad have stuff to do in town, so they can't drive us to the rec center," he said. "But I can walk with you two to practice. We'll just need to leave in the next ten minutes so I can get to my soccer scrimmage. I'll wait in the living room."

"Ah, man! We were having so much fun. I almost forgot we had practice," Asiyah said. She looked at her phone. "Maybe we can watch the video one more time . . ."

But Lucy shook her head. "We should probably get ready so we can walk with Rad."

"Why do we even have practice on Saturdays?" Asiyah asked. "We've already practiced so much. Plus, we just do the same things over and over. It gets kind of boring."

"But working on the same skills helps us get better," Lucy said. "When we play against a tough team, we'll be glad we practiced so much."

"I suppose," Asiyah said. "But you know me, I like doing different things. I just want to have fun!"

"Seriously, Asiyah," Lucy said, frowning. "You are good at making things fun, but everyone has to work hard in practice. You don't want to let your teammates down by not being prepared."

Asiyah sighed and started gathering her volleyball gear. *But I haven't let people down. I'm the one keeping things light and fun!* she thought. *Isn't* that *part of being on a team?*

CHAPTER FIVE

Hurt Feelings

At the start of Saturday's practice,
Coach Elise called everyone together.

"Since our first game is a week away,
we're going to scrimmage today," she said.
"It's important to treat it like a real game,
so we can see what we need to work on."

Coach Elise split the girls into two groups.
She put Asiyah and Lucy on different teams.
Asiyah was in the front row, next to the net.
Lucy was right across from her.

Asiyah made some goofy faces at her friend. But Lucy didn't react. Instead, she looked very serious.

As everybody was getting to their spots, Asiyah turned around. "Shivani! Rachel! You guys have to see a music video that Lucy and I were watching. The singer had some great moves," she said. "Watch this."

Asiyah twirled around like the singer.

"Nice!" Shivani said.

"Thanks. I can show you how to do it," Asiyah added. "It's really easy."

Asiyah was about to spin again when Coach Elise blew her whistle. "Give us your full attention, please, Asiyah. Caroline is about to serve."

"Sorry, Coach! I'm completely ready," Asiyah replied.

Asiyah continued to sway back and forth as the serve came. The ball sailed straight to the back row. Rachel bumped it up high.

Using her fingertips, Shivani pushed the ball straight into the air. She set it perfectly for Asiyah to hit. Asiyah ran toward the ball, jumped up, and brought her hand down hard.

But she hit the ball off the side of her hand. It flopped over the net.

Lucy was right there to block it. She jumped and slammed it back onto Asiyah's side. No one could get to the ball. One point for Lucy's team.

Asiyah shook out her arms and legs. She moved her shoulders up and down. *OK, time to focus*, she told herself. *I won't let Lucy stop my attack like that again.*

But Asiyah couldn't help bopping to the music in her head as the next serve flew toward them.

Jessica slid on her knees and got under the ball. It was a great dig. Shivani then set it to the left of Asiyah.

But Asiyah wasn't in the right spot. She hadn't been paying close attention to where Shivani was putting the ball. Asiyah rushed over. She hit the ball, but she barely managed to get it over the net.

Lucy was ready. She smacked the ball down. Asiyah couldn't set up in time to block the shot.

THUNK! The ball hit the court.

"Yikes!" Asiyah said. "I've already let in two points."

"That's why we have to keep practicing," Lucy said from the other side of the net.

Asiyah could feel her face get hot. Lucy sounded more like a teacher scolding her than a friend. It was a little embarrassing.

Lucy's team scored more and more points. It wasn't until the score was 6–0 that Asiyah's team finally got a ball past Lucy and the other blockers.

Jessica pounded the serve for Asiyah's team. On the other side, Caroline set the ball. Lucy sent it spinning back over.

Rachel bumped it up. Asiyah smacked the ball, but she hit it way too hard. It flew toward the sidelines.

"It's going out!" Lucy yelled to her teammates. "Don't touch it!"

The ball bounced hard off the floor—about six inches outside the court. Lucy's team had scored another point.

Asiyah let out a frustrated sigh. *I just can't do anything right today,* she thought.

Coach Elise blew her whistle. "Girls, take a water break," she said. "Then we'll go over what we can improve."

Asiyah walked to the bleachers to grab her water bottle. Lucy, Shivani, and Jessica were gathered around a nearby water fountain. The girls couldn't see Asiyah because she was blocked by the stands. But Asiyah could hear them talking about practice.

"What's up with Asiyah today?" Shivani asked. "I mean, she's so funny and upbeat, like always. But it doesn't seem like her head is in the game."

Jessica nodded. "I noticed that too," she said. "It seemed like Asiyah was just trying to make us laugh during the scrimmage."

"Yeah. Like the way she was dancing between points," Shivani added. "It was distracting. She's not taking anything seriously."

Asiyah's heart sank. She did like to clown around, but she didn't want anyone to think the team wasn't important to her.

I'm sure Lucy will stand up for me, Asiyah thought. *She knows that even though I like to have fun, I want to do my best for the team.*

"Yeah, I don't get it. Asiyah could be a great player," Lucy said. "She just has to learn to focus and get more into the practices. We're all working our hardest. I wish she did too."

Asiyah didn't want to hear any more. She hurried toward the water fountain on the other side of the gym.

How could Lucy say that? Asiyah thought. *I might have complained about practices, but that doesn't mean I haven't been serious. It doesn't mean I don't care about the team.*

Asiyah sat down on a bench. She thought more about what her best friend had said. It wasn't too different from what Lucy had told her before practice. But it still hurt her feelings.

Maybe I should tell Lucy I overheard her, Asiyah thought.

Before Asiyah could do anything, Coach Elise blew her whistle. The break was over. Asiyah hesitated, then jogged back onto the court.

The scrimmage started again. This time, Asiyah stopped herself from wiggling and dancing. *Focus!* she told herself.

A few minutes later, Jessica was serving. She whacked the ball, but it hit the net. The ball bounced off, hit Shivani's shoulder, and landed right in Coach Elise's arms.

All the girls laughed—except Asiyah. Suddenly things weren't so funny anymore.

CHAPTER SIX

Tough Decisions

Right after practice, Asiyah rushed over to Rad. He was waiting by the doors. She was glad Lucy was getting a ride home with her parents. Asiyah didn't feel like talking anymore.

"How was practice?" Rad asked as they headed out. "Did it go well?"

"No, not really," Asiyah mumbled. "I overheard Lucy and some of the girls. They were saying my head wasn't in the game. It really hurt my feelings."

"I'm sorry, sis. That's tough," Rad replied. Then he paused. "But you know . . . you have been complaining about practices lately. And you're usually more about having fun than staying super focused."

Asiyah frowned. "I've just been trying to have some fun playing volleyball with my friends! And trying to make sure everyone else has fun too!" she exclaimed. "What's wrong with that?"

"Nothing," Rad said. "But maybe your teammates were already having fun by playing hard. Maybe being silly was sidetracking everyone else."

"I guess. Although now I'm not sure I'm even good enough to play on the team," Asiyah said. "Today, Lucy blocked me about seven times."

"Well, you need to decide if you want to put in the effort to get better," Rad replied. "If you don't, then maybe the travel team isn't right for you. And that's OK. You could always join the rec team again."

Asiyah looked down at the sidewalk. "Maybe I'm not cut out for the Panthers." She sniffed. "And it doesn't seem like the girls on the team have my back."

"Why don't you give it one more week?" Rad suggested. "Focus. Try your hardest. Then decide if it's for you."

"One more week," Asiyah said slowly. "I guess I could do that. I could push myself to be super focused and see if I like it."

At least then, she thought, *Lucy and the girls won't say that I didn't give one hundred percent.*

CHAPTER SEVEN

Going All Out

During the next week, Asiyah dedicated herself to each practice. She arrived early, warmed up before anyone else got there, and was ready to do any drill.

The work was tough, but Asiyah was committed to giving it her best shot.

By Thursday, Asiyah already noticed she was getting better at hitting the ball right in the center. It made her spikes more powerful. During one long drill, Asiyah was able to smack the ball hard onto the court.

Asiyah smiled. *Some drills are still a little boring, but I get why we have to do them,* she thought. *Practice really does make perfect!*

When the girls scrimmaged, Asiyah paid close attention to what everyone was doing. She was able to figure out where she should be standing when the ball was set. She was ready to help her teammates.

"Take a break, girls!" Coach Elise called.

As Asiyah walked off the court, the coach caught up with her. "Asiyah, you made some great hits earlier," she said. "Nice job coming straight at the ball."

"Thanks, Coach," Asiyah said. "I was watching how Lucy positioned herself when she had a couple kills the other day. It really helped. That and all the drills."

"Great! Keep it up," Coach Elise said.

Asiyah smiled. It felt good that the coach noticed she was improving.

Lucy and a few other girls walked over. "I heard my name!" she said.

"Oh, I was just telling Coach you're good at positioning yourself," Asiyah said. "Phew! I need some water." She panted like she was in a desert.

Even though Asiyah was taking practices seriously, she still wanted to be herself. That meant being a little silly sometimes.

Lucy followed Asiyah over to the water fountain. "Hey, do you want to come to my house after practice?" she asked. "I just watched the funniest video of a dog skateboarding. You have to see it!"

Asiyah looked at the floor. "Thanks, but I have a bunch of homework."

Lucy didn't say anything. She looked a little hurt.

"Plus, I have to practice for my next piano lesson," Asiyah added. She shrugged. "So much to do!"

"Oh . . . OK," Lucy said. "I guess I'll show you some other time." She gave Asiyah another extra-long look before walking away.

Asiyah sighed. She really did have homework and piano. But the truth was, she was still kind of upset with Lucy.

Besides, what would I even say to her? Asiyah thought. *I'll just stay out of Lucy's way. At least for now.*

CHAPTER EIGHT

Making Up

The next day was the Panthers' last practice before their first game. Asiyah had her best practice yet. She was making digs, blocking balls, and spiking well.

During a break, Asiyah walked over to the net. She wanted to spend extra time on a side blocking drill they had just learned.

She took a step to the side, turned, and jumped. *I'm so close to getting this right,* Asiyah thought. *I'll do it a few more times to make sure I'm ready for tomorrow's match.*

When she felt good, she went to grab her water bottle. Lucy, Shivani, and Jessica were sitting on the bleachers.

"Hey, we just saw you doing extra work," Lucy said. "Nice job out there!"

"Yeah, you really got the hang of that side block," Shivani added.

"Thanks!" Asiyah said. She walked back toward the court. Lucy followed behind.

"Asiyah, hold up a second," Lucy said.

Uh-oh. Has Lucy noticed that I've been avoiding her? Asiyah wondered. Then she said, "What's up?"

"You've been so quiet around me lately," Lucy said. "Is everything OK?"

Asiyah shrugged. "Everything's fine. I've just been focusing on volleyball."

"That's totally paid off," Lucy said.
"But . . . is something else going on?
It almost feels like you're mad at me."

I can't keep avoiding this, Asiyah thought.
I miss my friend. I have to talk to her sometime.

"Well," Asiyah started. "Last week,
I heard you, Shivani, and Jessica saying
that I needed to get more serious about the
team. It kind of hurt my feelings."

Lucy looked at her shoes. "Oh! I'm so
sorry. It's just that the other girls and I had
been working so hard, and it seemed like
you were goofing off. I got upset."

"I was only trying to make sure everyone
had fun," Asiyah said. "I really do care
about the team."

"I know you do. Can you forgive me?"
Lucy asked.

Asiyah was quiet, but then she nodded. "You're my best friend, no matter what. Plus, I get now that it's *not* fun when everyone is trying to focus and one person isn't. So I've been giving practices my best effort."

"It shows!" Lucy said. "You've already improved so much."

Asiyah smiled. "You know, at first I wasn't sure if the travel team was right for me. But I actually like pushing myself to get better. And I definitely don't want to let the team down."

Lucy hugged Asiyah. "You won't," she replied. "I can't wait to play our first game with you by my side."

"Me too," Asiyah said. She held out her hand for a high-five, and Lucy slapped it. "We'll be unstoppable travel-team buddies!"

CHAPTER NINE

First Game!

The next day, before their first home game against the Salisbury Fishercats, the Panthers went into the exercise room. They stretched quietly. Some girls were whispering about how tough the Fishercats were.

Asiyah looked around. *Everyone seems so tense,* she thought. *Is now the right time for fun?*

She made her decision. Asiyah ran back to the lockers and grabbed her phone. She burst into the exercise room and blasted the song she and Lucy had danced to earlier.

"Come on, everyone! Let's get pumped before the game!" Asiyah shouted.

For a second, the team stared at her. Asiyah gulped. But then the girls got up and started dancing.

"Panthers! Panthers!" the team chanted.

"This is the perfect way to get us going!" Lucy exclaimed.

Asiyah grinned. *It was a good time to loosen up after all!* she thought.

Soon Coach Elise walked in. She laughed when she saw her team dancing. "OK, girls! Five more minutes of fun. Then warm-ups."

After the song was finished, Asiyah went to put her phone away. Lucy followed her.

"All right," Asiyah said as she shut her locker. "Now it's time to get serious."

Lucy laughed. "Let's do this!"

The girls bumped fists and then ran onto the court.

* * *

The Fishercats team jogged out on the other side of the gym. Asiyah watched them as she ran through warm-ups.

Just looking at the Fishercats makes me nervous. They're tall! she thought. *And it'll be up to Lucy and me to block them. I hope I'm ready.*

Just then, Asiyah saw her mom, dad, and Rad walk in. They smiled and waved. Rad gave a thumbs-up. Asiyah did two thumbs-up back. She felt calmer already.

Soon the ref blew her whistle. Warm-ups were over. The girls got set up on the court. Lucy and Asiyah took their spots next to each other in the front row.

The Fishercats had the opening serve. Their player fired it over the net.

Shivani dropped to her knees and bumped it, but the ball didn't go very high. Asiyah wasn't expecting such a low pass. She got it before it hit the ground, but her shot didn't make it over the net.

Shake it off, Asiyah thought. *Keep focused.*

The Fishercats quickly scored three more points. But the Panthers broke the streak when Jessica whacked a ball right into the Fishercats' court. It was the Panthers' serve.

Jessica's serve sailed low over the net. The Fishercats setter set the ball up high. The tall redhead in front sent it flying back.

Rachel got her fist on it before it touched the ground. Then Jessica pushed the ball into the air.

Asiyah was ready. She took two steps, jumped up, and killed it!

Point to the Panthers! The girls ran together for high-fives.

"Nice moves, Asiyah!" Rachel said.

"That was your first kill of the season. That's so awesome!" Lucy said.

Asiyah felt really proud. *Now we just have to keep it going,* she thought.

The Panthers fired off more points. At 6–5, the Panthers lost the serve. The score began to seesaw back and forth.

Soon the score was 24–22. The Fishercats needed one more point to win the first set.

The Fishercats sent the ball over. Lucy immediately smashed it back. But a Fishercat in the back passed it to the setter.

Asiyah watched the setter. She seemed to be sending the ball to the redheaded girl. Asiyah and Lucy moved to block her.

But at the last second, another girl crossed over for the attack. Lucy and Asiyah weren't in the right position. The ball hit the ground.

The Fishercats had grabbed the first game, 25–22. But the match was the best of three games, so the Panthers could still win.

The Panthers walked off the court and huddled around Coach Elise. "Girls, you're playing really well," she said. "You talked to each other. You made good plays. Now go out there, and win this second set!"

"Let's do the Panthers cheer!" Asiyah shouted. "One, two, three . . ."

"Go, Panthers!" the girls yelled together. Then they ran back onto the court.

At the beginning of the second game, the Panthers showed off their power. They won the first eight points.

The Fishercats weren't about to give up. They brought the score back to 4–8. But after two quick kills by Lucy, the Panthers lengthened their lead.

From then on, the Panthers cruised. They won the second game by ten points.

"This is it. Whoever wins this next set, wins the game," Asiyah said to Lucy.

"We'll block whatever comes our way!" Lucy said as they switched sides of the court.

The girls fist bumped and got into their positions.

I've been practicing so hard, Asiyah thought. *I know I'm ready for anything in the third set.*

CHAPTER TEN

The Final Set

Both teams looked determined as the Fishercats got ready to serve. The final set was only up to fifteen points. It was important to score early.

The Fishercats grabbed the first point. But their server hit the next ball into the net. The Panthers got a point—and the serve.

Caroline tossed the ball into the air. She hit the serve so fast that the other team couldn't get under it. Ace!

After that, both teams battled hard. The score went back and forth. Before long, the score was tied, 13–13. It was the Fishercats' serve.

As the Panthers got ready, Asiyah noticed her teammates looked tense.

She clapped her hands, "Let's go, Panthers!" she shouted. "We can do this! Let's have some fun!"

The girls on the court smiled and nodded.

"Yeah, let's take it!" Lucy yelled.

The Fishercats' server smacked the ball.

"Mine!" Rachel yelled as she dove for it.

She dug the ball out and bumped it high. Shivani set it up. Lucy jumped and acted like she was going to hit it.

But at the last moment, Asiyah stepped over and hit the ball head on. It slammed down onto the Fishercats' side.

The Panthers scored! They led 14–13. They needed one more point to win the match.

Asiyah took a deep breath. *You're ready for this,* she told herself.

Jessica served the ball. The Fishercats' captain passed to the setter. She took a step over and prepared to send it to one of the hitters.

She's setting the ball for the redhead. I'm sure of it, Asiyah thought. *She's going to come in and hit it to the side.*

Asiyah set herself up for a side block. *Step, turn, and block,* she repeated in her head. She had worked so hard on this. She knew she'd be able to pull it off.

Asiyah was right. The redhead started to move, and Asiyah was ready. She jumped up to block the ball at the exact moment the Fishercat came down with it.

Asiyah smashed the ball back over the net. The Fishercats scrambled to get it, but the ball dropped to the floor.

It was game over, and the Panthers had won!

The girls ran together in the middle of the court. They cheered and jumped up and down.

Lucy hugged Asiyah. "Amazing job!" she shouted.

"You did great too, Luce!" Asiyah replied. "Wow, that was such an exciting game. You were right. It *is* fun playing tougher teams."

"You were definitely ready for the competition. The whole team was!" Lucy said. She grinned. "I'm happy you stuck with the Panthers."

Asiyah smiled back. "And I'm happy we're in this together."

Then Asiyah made two thumbs-up. Lucy laughed, and they both did the silly thumbs-up dance, glad that they were teammates.

Author Bio

Wendy L. Brandes writes books for children, including Capstone's Summer Camp series. Wendy played volleyball in middle school and during her freshman year of high school. She loved to serve. But her favorite part of volleyball was sliding on the floor (in kneepads) to dig out a tough shot!

Illustrator Bio

Katie Wood fell in love with drawing when she was very small. Since graduating from Loughborough University School of Art and Design in 2004, she has been living her dream working as a freelance illustrator. From her studio in Leicester, England, she creates bright and lively illustrations for books and magazines all over the world.

Glossary

competitive (kuhm-PEH-tuh-tiv)—wanting to win or be the best at something

court (KORT)—the playing area in volleyball

dedicate (DED-uh-keyt)—to give something (such as your time and full attention) to a special cause or goal

drill (DRIL)—a repetitive exercise that helps you learn a specific skill

hijab (hi-JAHB)—a covering for the head worn by Muslim women

improve (im-PROOV)—to become better

Muslim (MUHZ-luhm)—someone who follows the religion of Islam

scrimmage (SKRIM-ij)—a practice game, often played between two groups from the same team

squad (SKWAHD)—a sports team

Discussion Questions

1. How would you describe Asiyah's personality? Use examples from the story to support your answer.

2. In your own words, summarize why Lucy and the other girls were feeling frustrated with Asiyah. How else could Lucy have dealt with her feelings toward Asiyah's work? Discuss some other options.

3. Asiyah thinks about quitting the team, but Rad convinces her to give it another week. Talk about a time you almost gave up on something, but didn't. How did it feel?

Writing Prompts

1. Write a list of Asiyah's "Tips for Success." Think about what she learned that could apply to any challenge, not just sports.

2. A travel team requires more commitment than a rec team, but it offers a chance to play tougher games and improve. Which team would you want to be on? Write two paragraphs arguing for your choice.

3. Asiyah and Lucy have a strong friendship. They were able to work through their problems. Write about your best friend. How are you two alike? How are you different?

Volleyball Terms

ACE—a serve that the other team can't return; an ace results in a point for the serving team

BLOCK—a defensive play where a player puts her hands up to stop a ball from coming over the net

BUMP—a pass using joined forearms

CARRY—when a player almost scoops the ball and touches it for too long; carrying is not allowed

DIG—to dive for a fast ball and hit it before it touches the floor

KILL—a successful spike attack; when you kill the ball, your team gets a point

RALLY—a series of shots between teams before a point is won

SERVE—the first hit used to put the ball into play; serves are aimed at the other team's side of the net

SET—a high pass that puts the ball in a position to be spiked, often done overhead using the fingertips

SPIKE—a hard, overhead, one-handed hit meant to send the ball down on the other side of the net; also called an attack

TIP—a soft, one-handed hit where a player controls the ball with her fingertips; a tip is supposed to lightly send the ball to the other side of the net